First published in Great Britain in 2002 by Brimax
An imprint of Octopus Publishing Group Ltd
2-4 Heron Quays, London E14 4JP

© 1997 bohem press, Zurich, Switzerland

ISBN 1 85854 457 2

Printed in China

A CIP catalogue record for this book is available from the British Library.

Little Star

Written and illustrated by

Arcadio Lobato

BRIMAX

J206,206 €12.00

One clear summer night in a sleepy little village,
frogs croaked and crickets chirped.

While a little girl named Helen got ready for bed, warm lights glowed in the open windows of her house and hundreds of stars sparkled brightly in the night sky.

After Helen snuggled under the covers, her mother read her a fairy tale, as she did every night.

"Once upon a time, there was a beautiful princess," her mother began. As she read, the words floated up over the trees and through the night sky to the clouds.

High above, shining with a soft, blue light, Little Star listened carefully to the story.

This night's story was about a princess who lived in a golden palace. She had riches beyond imagining, the finest clothes in all the land, and even a herd of elephants. But the princess's greatest wish was to pick a star from the sky and keep it for her very own.

Little Star listened to the tale in wonder. By the end of the story, Helen had fallen sound asleep.

Little Star didn't understand that it was just a bedtime story. He dreamed of meeting the princess, visiting the palace, and seeing the herd of elephants. He wanted to be the star that the princess plucked from the night sky.

Little Star slipped away from the larger stars who watched over him. Following the echo of Helen's mother's words, he floated gently to earth.

Helen woke up to find a soft blue light shining in her eyes.
It was a tiny star, just outside her bedroom window. "I must
be dreaming," said Helen, rubbing her eyes.

"Hello, Princess," said Little Star, twinkling as he spoke.
"I have found you at last! I am the star you wished for. Please
will you show me your palace, your fine clothes, and your
herd of elephants?"

Helen frowned. "I'm not a princess, I'm just an ordinary
little girl, in an ordinary house. My name is Helen."

"So you aren't the princess?" Little Star began to cry blue,
sparkly tears.

Helen felt sorry for the star and longed to cheer him up.
"I know!" she said. "I'll be Princess Helen just for tonight
and show you my kingdom. Come with me."

Helen wrapped her blanket around her shoulders. It floated behind her like a velvety cloak. For Little Star, she had become the beautiful princess from the story. Helen led Little Star through the sleepy village.

Helen greeted the croaking frogs, the singing crickets, the glow-worms, and a neighbour's cat as if she owned all the land.

"These are my loyal subjects," Helen told Little Star.

"And this is my golden palace." Helen pointed to a big building. Lights glowed from the windows and flowers decorated the window boxes.

"It's beautiful," said Little Star.

Since there were no elephants in Helen's neighbourhood, she led Little Star to the goats and pigs that lived nearby.

"These are the animals that live in my kingdom," said Helen.

"What wonderful creatures," said Little Star, happily.

Suddenly, a bright red light floated down from the night sky.
It was a very large star and it did not look pleased. Helen took
a step backwards and clutched her blanket.

"What are you doing down here, Little Star?" asked the red
star sternly. "You know that stars cannot leave the sky. You
must come back home now."

"But why?" cried Little Star. "I am having so much fun here with Princess Helen. I am the star she wished for, and I want to stay."

"I'm afraid that is not possible," explained the older and wiser star.

"Your place is in the sky with the rest of the stars.
We need you to help us light up the night."

But Little Star did not want to return home.

Helen knew the red star was right, so she came up with a plan.

"Come here, Little Star," she said. "I have to tell you a secret."
Little Star eagerly followed her around the corner of the house.
As Helen whispered her secret, Little Star began to shine
brighter and brighter.

"Well, if that is true, Princess, then I must return to the sky."

So Little Star and the wise red star drifted back up to the sky.

"Goodbye, Helen," called Little Star.

"Goodbye, Little Star," replied Helen.

As Helen climbed back into bed, Little Star looked down from above, sparkling like a diamond. The red star glowed next to him.

"What did Princess Helen say to make you change your mind?" asked the red star.

"She has a special job for me," explained Little Star. "I'm supposed to light up the night sky for the frogs, the crickets, the goats, the pigs, and all the creatures in her kingdom. My light is what gives her palace its golden glow."

"That's a big job," said the red star. "You'll have to stay up here all the time."

"I know," said Little Star, proudly. "But this is where stars belong, isn't it?"

On clear summer nights, when crickets chirp and frogs croak, bedtime stories echo in the air. As little girls fall asleep, the stars high above listen to these stories and watch over their dreams.

And Little Star shines especially bright. He is keeping watch over a very special princess and her kingdom because he knows that sometimes fairy tales really can come true.